Blue

Music

Beginning

Listen

Strings

To our oral storytellers – for it is they who keep our imagination alive.
My thanks to Sonia, Alex, Bárbara and Guillermo for helping me to
construct this story.
G.

First published in English in 2017 by order of the Tate Trustees
by Tate Publishing, a division of Tate Enterprises Ltd,
Millbank, London SW1P 4RG
www.tate.org.uk/publishing

First published in Spanish as 'Érase'
©2016 Raúl Nieto Guirdi
©2016 Ediciones TTT
Translation rights arranged through the VeroK Agency,
Barcelona, Spain
All rights reserved for all countries, www.testigrestristes.com
Translated by Alayne Pullen in association with First Edition Translations Ltd,
Cambridge, UK.

English translation ©2017 Tate Enterprises Ltd.

A catalogue record for this book is available from the British Library
ISBN 978 1 84976 513 8
Distributed in the United States and Canada by ABRAMS, New York

Library of Congress Control Number applied for
Printed in China by C&C Offset Printing Co., Ltd.

Once upon a time

From the very beginning, as soon as he
was born, Bard loved words.

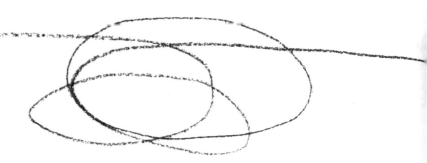

As he grew up he started making sentences out of these words, and paragraphs from those sentences and with these paragraphs he transformed the most ordinary situations into unforgettable stories for the people who lived in his village.

Platypus

Kaleidoscope

Whenever they could, the villagers would come to Bard with new words, hoping to get him to tell them an exciting story. They gave him the strangest words they could think of such as 'PLATYPUS' and 'KALEIDOSCOPE'. They gave him hundreds and thousands of synonyms and millions and billions of adjectives.

Bard would transform their words into stories that carried
them all away to extraordinary places.

But one morning, just like any other, when no one was expecting it . . .

Bard stopped speaking.

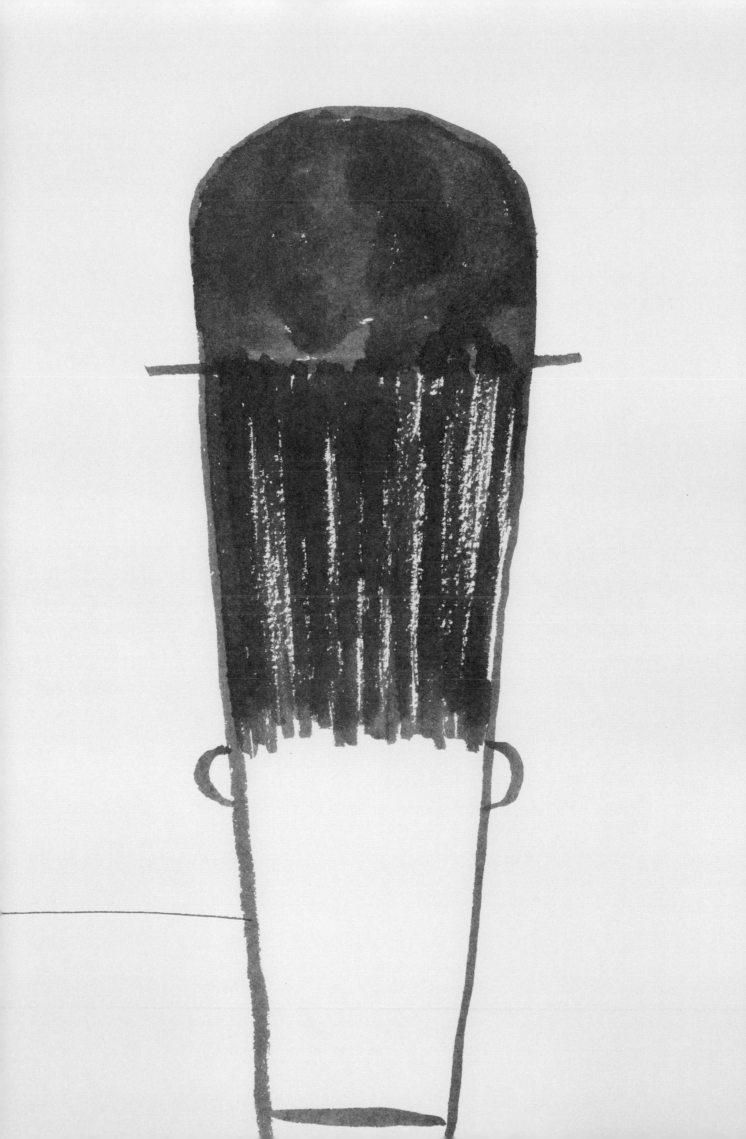

The villagers couldn't believe it.
Some thought that it was the end of the world.
Others blamed each other without really knowing why.
And the doctor said it was a twenty-four-hour virus . . .

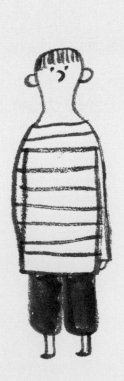

But it wasn't . . .
Forty-eight hours later things were still the same.

There was silence.

Silence.

And more silence.

The days went by but Bard didn't
utter a single word.

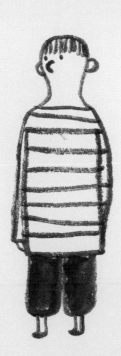

"Is he upset?" asked the mayor.
"He is angry!" claimed the teacher.
"No, he is bamboozled," the priest said firmly.
"He must be in love," said the old lady, who was
always getting things wrong.
"It's all too much," the baker declared.
"Oh goodness! Oh gosh!" Everyone cried out.

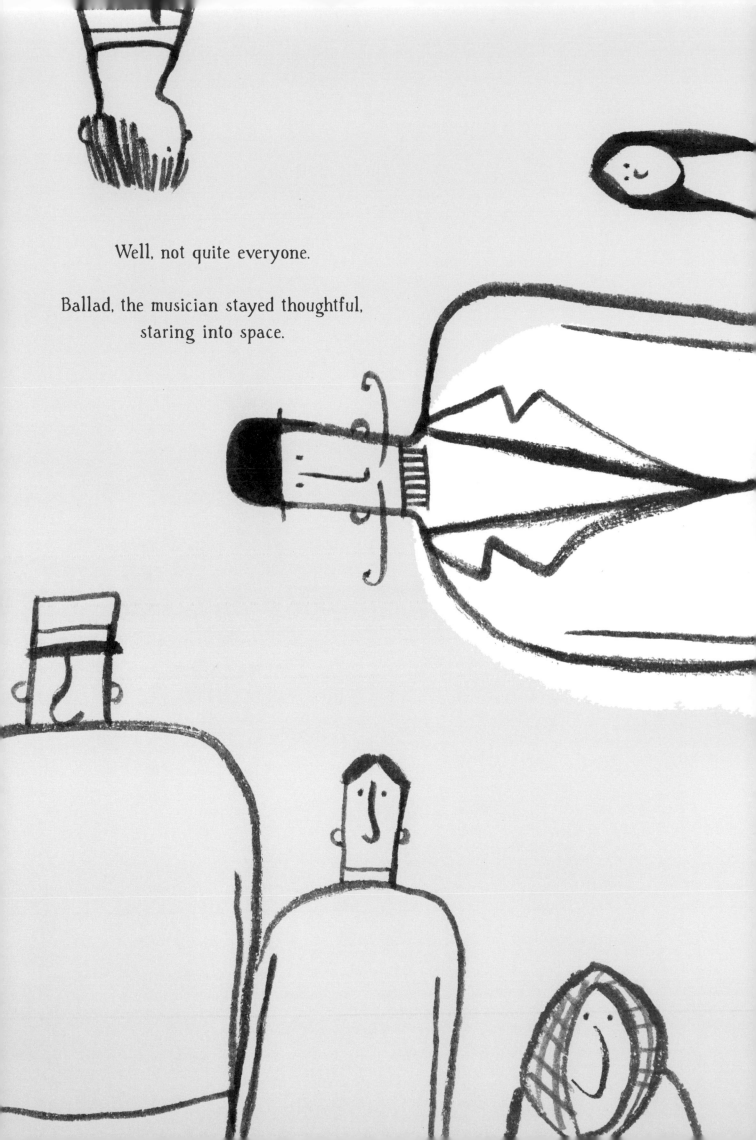

Well, not quite everyone.

Ballad, the musician stayed thoughtful,
staring into space.

The mood in the village was very blue. How were they going to live without stories? No one knew what to do. Some tried to tell their own stories but the words didn't fit or wouldn't come out.

But Bard remained silent.

Some were sure that if they dressed up like storybook characters,
Bard would find the words to start telling his stories again.

"This is ridiculous!" said the others as they
put on their costumes.

But still Bard remained silent.

They wanted to give him new words, as they had always done, but the only words they could come up with were 'DULL', 'BOREDOM' and 'SADNESS'.

It seemed that nothing could be done to make Bard tell
stories again.

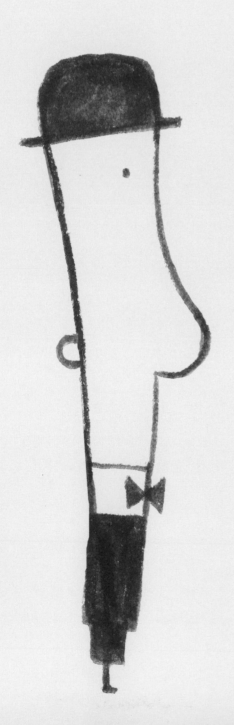